THE BALL BOUNCED

NANCY TAFURI

GREENWILLOW BOOKS · NEW YORK

One day

the ball

bounced.

The cat jumped.

The water

splashed.

The dog ran.

The ball rolled.

The door

slammed.

The bird flew.

The dog barked.

The ball stopped.

And the

baby laughed!

FOR ALLIE

Library of Congress Cataloging-in-Publication Data
Tafuri. Nancy.   The ball bounced / by Nancy Tafuri.   p.   cm.
Summary: A bouncing ball causes much excitement around the house.
ISBN 0-688-07871-0.   ISBN 0-688-07872-9 (lib. bdg.)
[1. Balls (Sporting goods) — Fiction.]   I. Title.   PZ7.T117Bal 1989
[E] — dc19   87-37582   CIP   AC